BIG LONELY DOG

by

LEONORE
HARRIS

pictures by *DOROTHY ALLYN DEETS*

HOUGHTON MIFFLIN COMPANY
The Riverside Press Cambridge
1943

All the People and Dogs in this book are
real and any resemblance to any living
Person or Dog is purely intentional.

To Hamlet's most admiring public:

Carl, Arthur, and Hildegarde

Once there was a big lonely dog who lived in a kennel with many other dogs. He was lonely because he didn't have any People. He wanted to live in a house with People who would give him a name and rub him behind his ears and pet him. Most of all, he wanted to have some People to WATCH.

This big lonely dog was a Great Dane. He was born to be a WATCHING dog and so he was unhappy all the time because he had no People to WATCH. Sometimes he howled himself to sleep at night because he was so unhappy.

One evening a car drove up to the kennel and three People got out — Father, Mother, and their little boy, David.

The big lonely dog heard Father say to the kennel man, "I want a good WATCHING dog, maybe a Doberman Pinscher."

Mother said, "I want a nice LITTLE pet, maybe a Boston Bull."

David said, "I want a dog to PLAY with."

The kennel man said, "We have lots of dogs. Now here is a fine Doberman — tough as anything — and here's a cute Boston, Petunia-out-of-Champion-Snubby-Nose.   Or, how do you like this playful little Dachshund?"

"I will make the People look at *me*," the big lonely dog growled to himself. And so he stood up on his back feet and he put his front feet on top of the high fence and he woofed and he woofed and he woofed. He made such loud noises that Father, Mother, and their little boy, David, ran right over to see him.

"He's certainly big," said Father.

"He's surely beautiful," said Mother.

"He's the color of honey," said David. "Does he bite?"

The kennel man said, "Yes, he's big and yes, he's beautiful and no, he doesn't bite — he's as GENTLE as a KITTEN. But, he is also the finest WATCHING dog you could buy. Nothing would ever happen to the People he lived with!"

The two big People talked to each other for a few moments and then they said, "We'll take him."

"Let's call him 'Hamlet,'" said Father. And they did.

"Oh, dear," said Mother when they got home, "whatever are we going to do with such a *big* dog?" Hamlet *was* big. He was higher than the dining room table and longer than the fireplace in the living room.

"Tomorrow we'll see," said Father. "Let's go to bed."

"This is a wonderful place," Hamlet said to himself, letting out just a small woof. "A big warm house with thick rugs all over and soft sofas to lie on and the smell of fine food. I must try to be a very GOOD dog and the best WATCHING dog there ever was."

The next morning when the People came down-stairs the first thing they saw was a big hole in a corner of the red rug.

"Oh, dear," said Mother, "whatever are we going to do about a dog who chews holes in the rug?"

Father said, "I will not HAVE a dog who chews holes in the rug.

Hamlet must go!

I love dogs

And Mother loves dogs

And David loves dogs

But Hamlet must GO!"

And their little boy David cried:

"OH, NO!"

So Hamlet stayed another day.

The next morning when the People came downstairs they found the door to the ice box open! And on the floor were the remains of a leg of lamb, a dozen eggs, a pound of bacon, a lemon cream pie, a bunch of bananas, and a bowl of pudding.

"Oh, dear," said Mother, "whatever are we going to do about a dog who eats us out of house and home?"

Father said, "I will not HAVE a dog who chews holes in the rug and eats us out of house and home.

Hamlet must go!

I love dogs

And Mother loves dogs

And David loves dogs

But Hamlet must GO!"

And their little boy David cried:

"OH, NO!"

So Hamlet stayed another day.

The next morning when the People came down-stairs they found that the long mirror which used to hang in the hall, was on the floor. It had been smashed to pieces.

"Oh, dear," said Mother, "whatever are we go-ing to do about a dog who breaks mirrors looking at himself?"

Father said, "I will not HAVE a dog who chews holes in the rug and eats us out of house and home and breaks mirrors looking at himself.

Hamlet must go!
I love dogs
And Mother loves dogs
And David loves dogs
But Hamlet must GO!"

And their little boy David cried:
"OH, NO!"

So Hamlet stayed another day.

The next morning when the People came downstairs they didn't find ANYTHING.

They   looked

          all   around

     in

     all   the

                         rooms

and they didn't find ANYTHING that Hamlet had done during the night.

Father was so pleased about this that he gave Hamlet a crust from his breakfast toast. Mother was so pleased about this that she gave Hamlet HALF her breakfast toast. David was so pleased about this that he gave Hamlet ALL his breakfast toast.

And then the doorbell rang.

When Father went to see who was at the door, there stood a POLICEMAN!

"Good morning," said the policeman. "Sorry, but we have THREE things against your dog.

"First, the dog jumped on your milkman . . . just a FRIENDLY jump, but he broke three bottles of milk.

"Second, the dog jumped on your newsboy . . . just a FRIENDLY jump, but he scattered a bagful of papers all over the street.

"Third, the dog jumped on your postman . . . just a FRIENDLY jump, but he threw the mail all over your yard.

"I am sorry, Sir, but if your BAD dog doesn't start to be a GOOD dog pretty soon he will have to come and live in our DOG-HOUSE at the jail.   Good-day, Sir."

"Oh, dear," said Mother, "whatever are we going to do about a dog who jumps on the milkman, the newsboy, and the postman?"

Father said, "I will not HAVE a dog who chews holes in the rug and eats us out of house and home and breaks mirrors looking at himself and jumps on the milkman, the newsboy, and the postman. TOMORROW, HAMLET GOES BACK TO THE KENNEL!

Go, go, Hamlet must go!
I love dogs
And Mother loves dogs
And David loves dogs
But Hamlet must GO!"

And their little boy David cried:
"OH, NO!"

Father's answer to that was easy to guess.

"Oh, yes!" was his answer.

"THIS TIME, YES!"

Hamlet didn't sleep a wink all night. Early in the morning, when he saw the sun rising, he felt sadder and lonelier than he had ever felt in all his life.

"Why," he woofed silently, "oh, why did I have to be such a bad dog? Why did I have to chew holes in the rug and eat them out of house and home and break a mirror looking at myself and jump at the milkman, the newsboy, and the postman?"

Before Hamlet had a chance to answer himself, something HAPPENED. A big drop of water splashed on his neck. He jumped up! Another drop of water splashed on his tail. He looked around! Another drop of water splashed on his nose. He sniffed the air.

"Woof, woof!" he thought, scratching his head. "I wonder what's wrong!"

Drip-drip-drip came the water, splashing down steadily and fast. Hamlet's back was all wet now. He shook himself from head to tail and little drops of water hit the four walls. Little pools of water stood on the floor.

"This is bad," growled Hamlet. "My People wouldn't like it. They might think I did it. Woof, woof, I must TELL MY PEOPLE!"

Slipping and sliding on the wet floor, Hamlet ran to the hall. Leaping up the stairs four steps at a time, he came to the second floor. Then, he sniffed under all the closed doors until he found the room where the big People were sleeping.

"This is it," he thought, and he started calling from the bottom of his throat.

"Woof-woof woof-woof-woof!" he barked, but nobody came.

"Woo-woo-woo-woo-woo!" he howled, but nobody came.

"Woof-woof-woof! Woo-woo-wooooo!"

F-I-N-A-L-L-Y, Father came sleepily to the door in his pajamas and bathrobe. Mother came sleepily to the door in her nightgown and housecoat. Then, David came to *his* door. He was *very* surprised.

Father said, "I will not HAVE a dog who wakes us up so early in the morning after he has . . . after he has chewed holes in the rug and eaten us out of house and home and broken a mirror looking at himself and jumped on the milkman, the newsboy, and the postman. TODAY, Hamlet goes back to the kennel!"

David said, "Hamlet's all wet."

Mother said, "Goodness sake's alive, Hamlet's all wet."

Father said, "Ye gods and little fishes, Hamlet's all wet."

Hamlet ran to the staircase and pointed his nose down the stairs. Then he looked at his People and pointed his nose down the stairs. Then he looked at his People again and pointed his nose down the stairs. His tail was wagging sixty miles an hour.

Father said, "He's trying to tell us something."

Mother said, "He wants us to go downstairs."

David said, "Let's GO downstairs!"

Father, Mother, David, and Hamlet all raced downstairs as fast as they could. Hamlet won the race.

"It's a leak!" said Father when he saw the water dripping from the ceiling. "Call the plumber, dear!"

While Mother was calling the plumber, Father began to mop up the floor. He carried an umbrella to keep his head dry. David began to rub Hamlet with a bath towel and *he* carried his *little* umbrella to keep *his* head dry.

Then, the plumber came!

"Well, well, well," said the plumber. "Something must be wrong in your upstairs bathroom." And he hurried upstairs to stop the leak.

"It's all right now," called the plumber from upstairs, "but I got here JUST IN TIME. The pipe might have broken and let out ALL the water!"

"ALL the water would have hurt my grand piano," said Mother. "It was GOOD of Hamlet to tell us about the leak!"

"ALL the water would have hurt my red leather chair," said Father. "It was SMART of Hamlet to tell us about the leak!"

"ALL the water would have hurt my electric train," said David. "Maybe Hamlet will always tell us EVERYTHING!"

Then the plumber came downstairs and the first thing Hamlet did was to jump on the plumber . . . just a FRIENDLY jump, but he spilled all his tools.

The plumber didn't care! He rubbed Hamlet behind his ears and said, "My, what a wonderful dog! If you People ever want to part with him, I'd like him for a mascot. Want to come with me, Big Dog?"

"Oh, no!" cried Father.

"I love dogs
And Mother loves dogs
And David loves dogs
And HAMLET CAN'T GO!"

"Well, well, well," said the plumber, "he is certainly a beautiful BIG DOG."

"He is a beautiful BIG WATCHING DOG," said David. "HE WATCHES DAY AND NIGHT!"

From that time on, Hamlet felt just a little bigger than ever before. Never, never again was he ever going to feel lonely because now he knew that for the rest of his life he would always have People — PEOPLE TO WATCH.